Fast Friends

Heather M. O'Connor

illustrated by
Claudia Dávila

Scholastic Canada Ltd.

Toronto New York London Auckland Sydney
Mexico City New Delhi Hong Kong Buenos Aires

Scholastic Canada Ltd.
604 King Street West, Toronto, Ontario M5V 1E1, Canada

Scholastic Inc.
557 Broadway, New York, NY 10012, USA

Scholastic Australia Pty Limited
PO Box 579, Gosford, NSW 2250, Australia

Scholastic New Zealand Limited
Private Bag 94407, Botany, Manukau 2163, New Zealand

Scholastic Children's Books
Euston House, 24 Eversholt Street, London NW1 1DB, UK

www.scholastic.ca

Library and Archives Canada Cataloguing in Publication

Title: Fast friends / Heather M. O'Connor ; illustrated by Claudia Dávila.
Names: O'Connor, Heather, 1960- author. | Dávila, Claudia, illustrator.
Identifiers: Canadiana 20190201053 | ISBN 9781443170406 (softcover)
Subjects: LCSH: Friendship—Juvenile literature. | LCSH: Interpersonal
communication—Juvenile literature. | LCSH: Nonverbal communication in
children—Juvenile literature.
Classification: LCC HM1161 .O26 2020 | DDC j302.34083—dc23

6 5 4 3 2 1   Printed in Malaysia 108   20 21 22 23 24

Tyson did everything fast.
He printed fast.
He moved fast.
He ate fast.

It sometimes made him
knock over his chair.
Or the red paint.
Or the kids in his class.
His teacher was always saying,
"Too fast, Tyson!"

Recess was different.
Tyson could jump and climb
and race around the schoolyard
speedy-quick.

But he couldn't go outside until
everyone was ready.

Every day, Tyson had to wait.
And wait. And WAIT.
Some days he'd say, "Hurry up!"

7

Those days, Tyson
played alone.

HOW I **PICTURE** MY FUTURE SELF

NICO

Lisa

Krisha

Carlos

One day, a new kid joined the class.

"This is Suze," said the teacher.

Suze didn't say hello. She didn't smile. She didn't even look at anyone.

But she did look at the race car picture hanging on the wall. Tyson saw her. The car was red and shiny, just like her chair. And the driver wore a crash helmet, just like Suze.

At lunch, Tyson finished speedy-quick.
But Suze ate her lunch through a tube,
so she was even faster.

When Tyson reached for his favourite
book, Suze already had her eye on it.
"Want to read?" he asked.

When it was time to go outside, the teacher picked Raf to walk with Suze, even though Tyson's hand shot up first.

14

"Be careful, Raf. Walk slowly,"
said the teacher.
    Raf did. So slowly that Suze
took a snooze.

The next day, Tyson read to Suze
again. This time, the teacher picked
Lisa to walk with Suze.

Lisa watched the big kids play basketball.
Suze didn't.

On his way home after school,
Tyson heard, "Beep, beep!
Coming through."
   He jumped out of the way.
   A shiny red chair whizzed by,
speedy-quick. It was Suze!

A big girl was pushing
her. "Coming through,"
she shouted again.

19

Tyson caught up with them at the park.

He climbed on the swing beside Suze. "Race you!" He pumped as hard as he could.

"Want to go fast, Suze?"
asked the big girl.
Suze waved her arms.
"Faster?"
Suze smiled, big and wide.

When Suze and Tyson were all tuckered out, the big girl said, "Time to get my sister home. See you, Speedy."

She zipped off with Suze, shouting, "Beep, beep!"

The next day at recess, Tyson's hand was up in a flash. "Can I play with Suze?"

The teacher wore his frowny face. "Okay, Tyson. But be careful."

Tyson would be careful. But
he would be speedy-quick too.

"Start your engines, Suze!" And he raced her around the schoolyard.

Suze and Tyson zigzagged past the teachers on yard duty. "Beep, beep!"

The teachers shouted, "Too fast, Tyson! Slow down!" They rushed after Suze and Tyson.

Suze and Tyson raced past the kids in their class. "Beep, beep!"

The kids stopped playing, and they ran after Suze and Tyson too.

Suze and Tyson cut through the basketball court. "Coming through!"

The basketball players stopped shooting hoops and started chasing Suze and Tyson.

Then Tyson and the teachers and the kids and the basketball players all heard a new sound, one they'd never heard before.

It was Suze.

She was waving her arms and laughing — great big happy belly laughs.

Tyson grinned. He wasn't too fast. He was speedy-quick.

And that was just fast enough.